To Hamlet
(my guinea pig when I was
the same age as Pinky Dinky Doo),
and to Frisky
(my daughter's hamster).
Thank you for inspiring Mr. Guinea Pig.

Special thanks to Katonah Elementary School
and to Lewisboro Elementary School

Photography by Sandra Kress

Digital coloring and compositing by Paul Zdanowicz

Copyright © 2005 by Sesame Workshop and Cartoon Pizza, Inc. PINKY DINKY DOO and associated characters, trademarks, and design elements are owned and licensed by Cartoon Pizza, Inc., and Sesame Workshop. Sesame Workshop and its logos are trademarks and service marks of Sesame Workshop. All rights reserved under International and Pan-American Copyright Conventions. Published in the United States by Random House Children's Books, a division of Random House, Inc., New York, and simultaneously in Canada by Random House of Canada Limited, Toronto, in conjunction with Sesame Workshop.

www.stepintoreading.com

Educators and librarians, for a variety of teaching tools, visit us at
www.randomhouse.com/teachers

Library of Congress Cataloging-in-Publication Data
Jinkins, Jim.
Pinky Dinky Doo : back to school is cool! / written and illustrated by Jim Jinkins.
    p.   cm. — (Step into reading. A step 3 book)
SUMMARY: When her little brother, Tyler, is nervous about his first day of school, Pinky Dinky Doo tells him a story about the time she and her friends had really bad hair days when school pictures were scheduled.
ISBN 0-375-83236-X (trade) — ISBN 0-375-83237-8 (pbk.) — ISBN 0-375-93237-2 (lib. bdg.)
[1. Brothers and sisters—Fiction. 2. Storytelling—Fiction. 3. First day of school—Fiction.
4. Schools—Fiction. 5. Hair—Fiction.]
I. Title. II. Series.
PZ7.J57526Bac 2005 [E]—dc22 2004010476

Printed in the United States of America   10 9 8 7 6 5 4 3 2

STEP INTO READING, RANDOM HOUSE, and the Random House colophon are registered trademarks of Random House, Inc.

STEP INTO READING®

STEP 3

Pinky Dinky Doo

BACK TO SCHOOL IS COOL!

by Jim Jinkins

Random House 🏠 New York

It was the first day
back to school
from summer break.
"Back to school rules!"
Pinky shouted.
"Back to school drools,"
Tyler said.

"Come on, little brother,

time to get dressed," said Pinky.

"I'm not going," Tyler said.

He pulled the covers over his head.

"You are too," said Pinky.

"I am not," said Tyler.

"Tyler!

Hurry up,"

Mom shouted up the stairs.

"The big bus will be here soon!"

Tyler yelped and disappeared

somewhere in the laundry.

Pinky noticed that the clothes
were shaking.
"Wow, Tyler,
you're shaking like you're . . .
what's that word
that means you're
really nervous?
What's that
word that means
you're totally
worried?"

"Apprehensive?"

Tyler said from under the laundry.

"That's it!"

said Pinky.

"That's the word I'm looking for."

"So you're apprehensive about the first day in the first grade?" Pinky asked.

All Tyler could do was touch his nose— which anybody knows means Pinky was right on the nose.

Ap-ree-HEN-siv. The "a" sound is like the "a" sound in "apple."

Book of BIG WORDS

12

"That gives me an idea!"
said Pinky.
"Are you going to make up
one of your stories?"
Tyler asked.
"Yesserooni positooni!"
Pinky said.

13

"I'll just shut my eyes,

wiggle my ears,

and crank up my imagination,"

said Pinky.

"The name of this story is . . ."

It was a no-big-deal,
regular day at

Great Big School.

NOT!

GREAT BIG SCHOOL

It was

School Picture Day!

It was the only day
of the whole school year
when everyone wanted
to look their absolute best.

PHOTO DETECTIVE
GUESS WHICH PHOTO IS JIM JINKINS (AUTHOR) IN THE FIRST GRADE
CLUES
1. HE'S NOT A CAT.
2. HE'S NOT A CARTOON.
3. HE'S NOT WEARING A TIE.
4. HE'S UNDER A BEE.

The answer is #15.

But that morning,

when Pinky looked in the mirror,

her eyes nearly popped

out of her head!

Her hair looked like:

A A tornado
had hit it.

B Two cats had
had a fight
on her head.

C It was spooky
haunted.

D All of the above.

The answer is D.

And D stands for Pinky Dinky's

Big Bad Hair Doo!

That is definitely a Pinky Dinky Don't!

Pinky was worried
about having her picture taken
with such a bad hairdo!

But Pinky was not the sort
of person to lie down
when problems came up.
So she and Mr. G got busy.

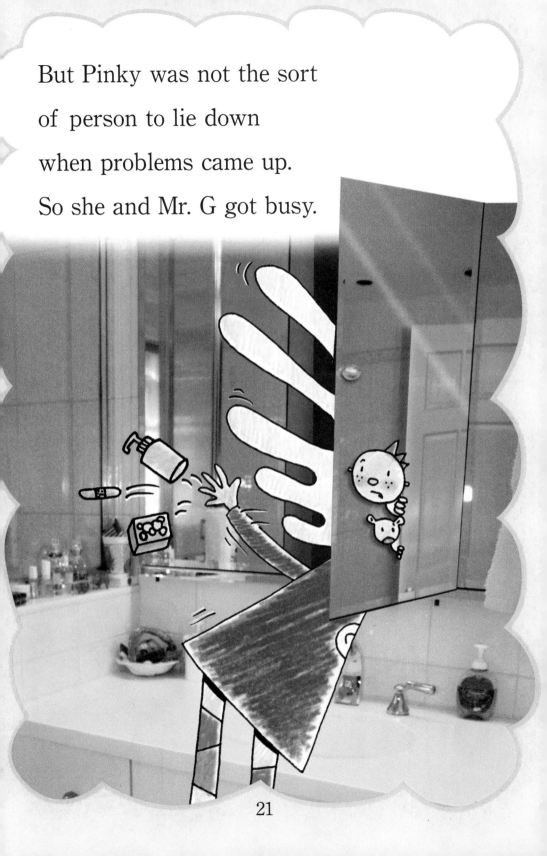

At first Mr. G
tried to pull
her hair up.

Then he tried
to comb
it down.

It worked for a second,
but then—

BOI-YOI-
YOING!

Finally,
Pinky decided that
she would have to wear a hat
to School Picture Day.

WOW!

So she spring-loaded
her Big Bad Hair
into a shiny hat.

At school,
Pinky noticed that
Nicholas Biscuit
was also wearing
a big hat.

The fake beard
made him look like
Abe Lincoln!

Normally,
Nicholas would comb
his hair into a pointy triangle.
But today his hair made
a quadrilateral.

Normally

"Quah-druh-LAT-er-ul"
"Quad" means "four" and
"lateral" means "with sides."

BOOK OF
BIG
WORDS

Today

Which shape is a quadrilateral?

A Underpants

B The Statue of Liberty

C A banana

D A rectangle

D! The answer is D!

Pinky looked around

for Daffinee Toilette.

"Daffinee will know what to do,"

Pinky said.

"Her hair is always perfect."

They found Daffinee.

Sure enough, her hair was perfect.

That is,

until she turned sideways.

Hey, she's wearing a cutout of perfect hair!

Behind the cutout
was a hairdo disaster.
It looked like Daffinee
was going 80 mph
while standing still!

"mph" means "miles per hour."

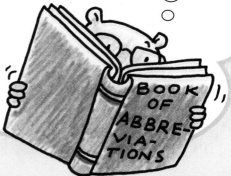

BOOK OF ABBRE-VIA-TIONS

When Pinky,
Nicholas,
and Daffinee
got to the classroom,
it looked empty.

Bobby "Broccoli-
head" Boom

Everyone was hiding
because they
were all having
a bad hair day.

Abby
McTrashy

Even Ms. Maganza and
Principal Dipthong
were having problems.

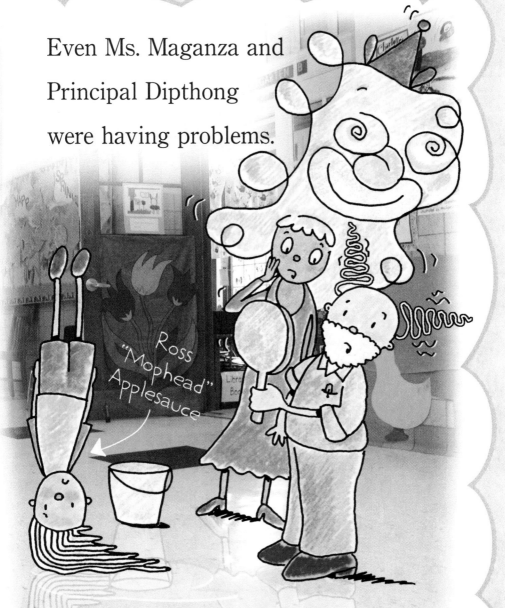

Ross
"Mophead"
Applesauce

And it was School Picture Day!
Everybody was reeeeally
apprehensive.

Pinky knew her friends were upset.

So she decided to Think Big!

Usually, Pinky had an everyday,

normal, kid-sized brain.

That is, until she decided to think big!

She thought

and thought

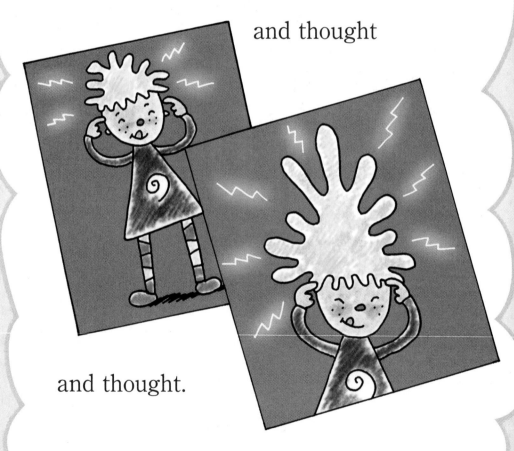

and thought.

This time as she thought,
her head didn't grow
any bigger at all . . .

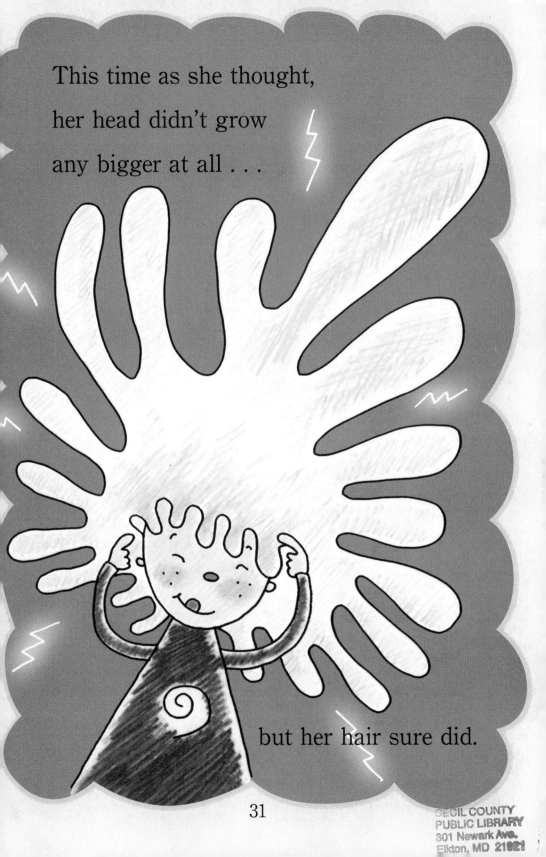

but her hair sure did.

31

Pinky Dinky's Hair Doo
grew bigger and
BIGGER and BIGGER
until the classroom
looked like
a shady rain forest.

And then it happened . . .

Pinky had a big idea.

She said,
"Hey, I know
what we can do . . .

A We can all shave our heads.

B We can knit our hair into

sweaters just in time for winter.

C We can just

GET OVER IT

and have our pictures

taken anyway!"

The answer was C, of course.

Everybody decided to just get over it and make the best of a bad hairdo situation.

They came out of hiding
and took off their hats
and hair cutouts.

Hey! I know
that birdy!

Then they marched
to the gym,
where Mr. Pixel was waiting
to take their school picture.

And just as you might have guessed, that class picture was the funniest class picture ever taken.

Nobody ever expected
to end up laughing on
a Bad Hair Day.
But they did.
And nobody
was apprehensive
ever again.

POOF!

"And that's *exactly* what happened . . . pretty much."

BEEP! BEEP! BEEP!

"Hey, that's the school bus,"
said Pinky.

"Oh no," Tyler said.

"I don't want to go on the bus!"

"Come on, Tyler," Pinky said.

"You can sit next to me.

We ride the big school bus

together, remember?"

"Oh yeah," Tyler said happily.

"Hurry up . . . ,"
said Pinky.

"Last one on the bus has

Big Bad Hair!"